Mr. Wiggle
Looks for
Answers

By Carol Thompson
Illustrated by Bobbie Houser

WATERBIRD BOOKS

Columbus, Ohio

This product has been aligned to state and national organization standards using the Align to Achieve Standards Database. Align to Achieve, Inc., is an independent, not-for-profit organization that facilitates the evaluation and improvement of academic standards and student achievement. To find how this product aligns to your standards, go to www.MHstandards.com.

Children's Publishing

This edition published in the United States of America in 2003 by Waterbird Books,
an imprint of McGraw-Hill Children's Publishing,
a Division of The McGraw-Hill Companies
8787 Orion Place
Columbus, Ohio 43240-4027

www.MHkids.com

Library of Congress Cataloging-in-Publication Data is on file with the publisher.

Printed in the United States of America.

1-57768-615-2

1 2 3 4 5 6 7 8 9 10 PHXBK 09 08 07 06 05 04 03

I am Mr. Wiggle, the library "know it all."
If you'll turn the page for me, I'll explain it all.

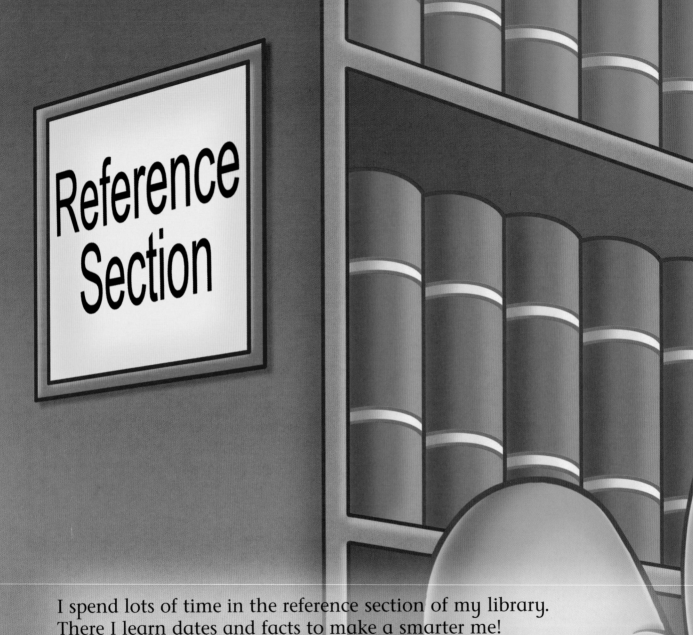

I spend lots of time in the reference section of my library.
There I learn dates and facts to make a smarter me!
Reference books are different from the ones I usually check out.
They can't be taken home with me, and research is all they're about.

5

ALMANAC

Thesaurus

CTIONARY

ATLAS

There are books called an atlas, an almanac, and thesaurus, too.
I'm just about to bust because I'm so anxious to show you!
There's also an encyclopedia and another book, a dictionary.
You can't even imagine how very helpful they will be.

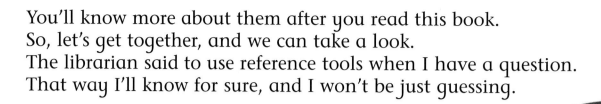

You'll know more about them after you read this book.
So, let's get together, and we can take a look.
The librarian said to use reference tools when I have a question.
That way I'll know for sure, and I won't be just guessing.

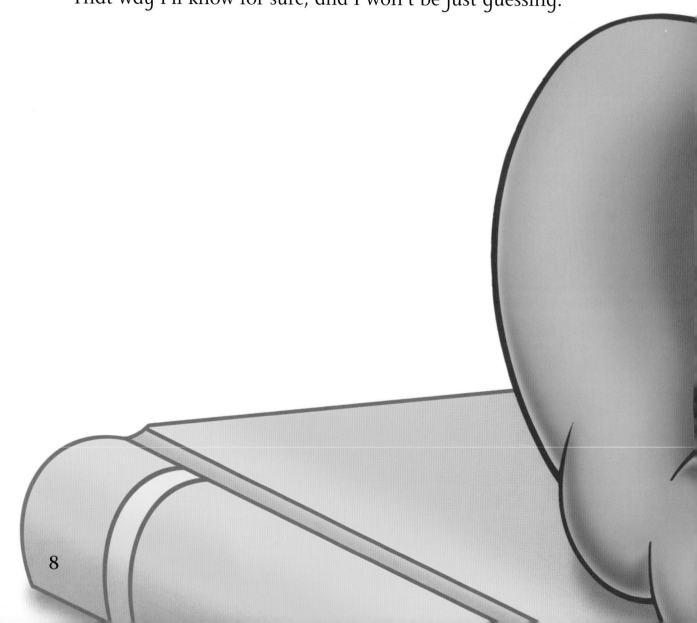

Here is the dictionary—a very interesting book.
If a word confuses you, I suggest you give it a look.
Inside you'll find every word from *A* all the way to Z.
And you'll learn how to spell it right, try it and you'll see!

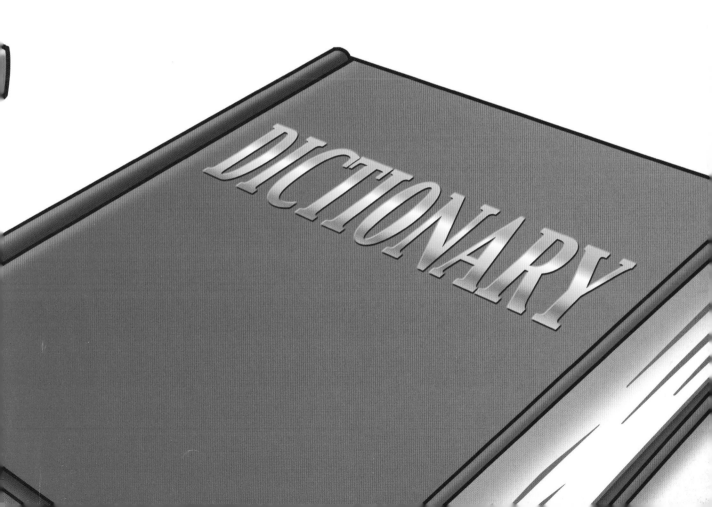

A dictionary also provides important information.
For any word, it gives a definition and pronunciation.
But when I need to look at a map, it's an atlas that I need.
The charts and graphs help me understand the maps I must read.

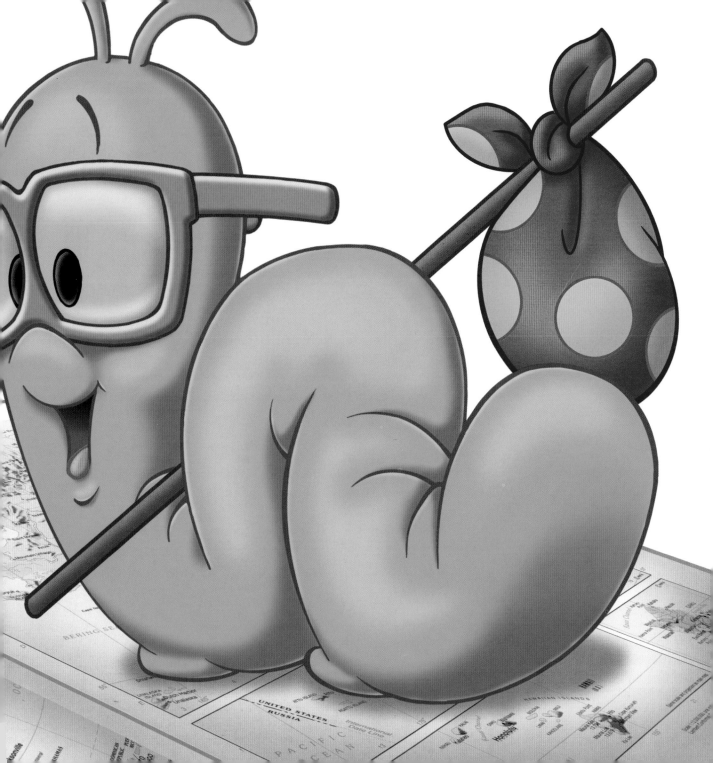

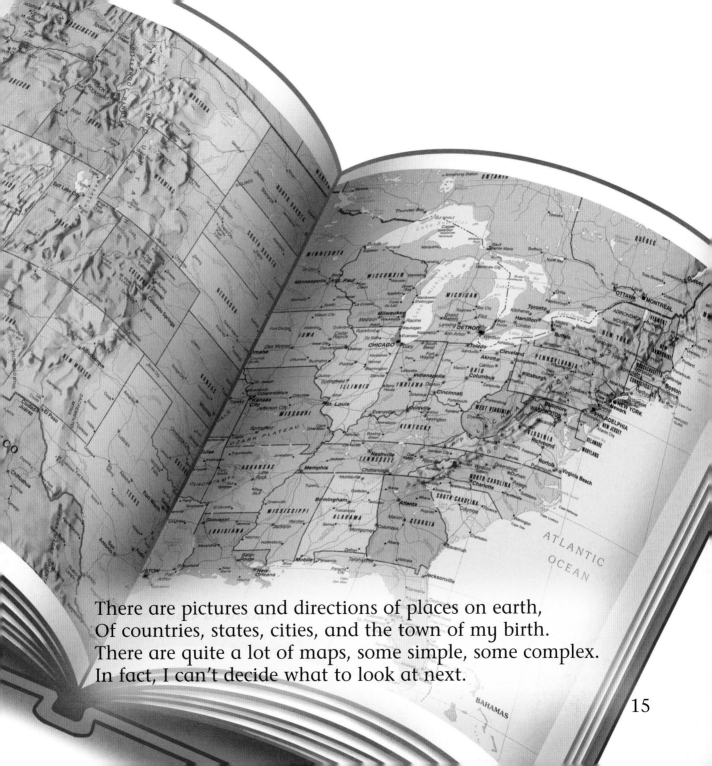

There are pictures and directions of places on earth,
Of countries, states, cities, and the town of my birth.
There are quite a lot of maps, some simple, some complex.
In fact, I can't decide what to look at next.

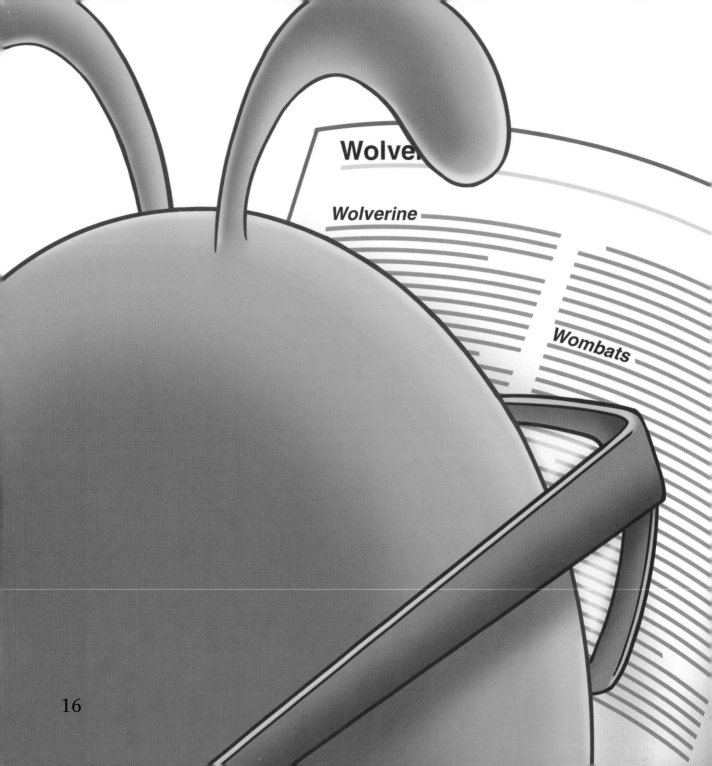

An encyclopedia holds information on many different topics.
It will tell you almost anything about an aspect of a subject.
To learn more about the word *worm*, in the *W*'s is where I'd look.
There I'll find all the facts and data I could want in this book.

It will tell me all the main points about worms like myself,
And when I'm finished, I will put it back on the shelf.
An almanac is an interesting book with many different sections.
A new one is printed every year with additions and corrections.

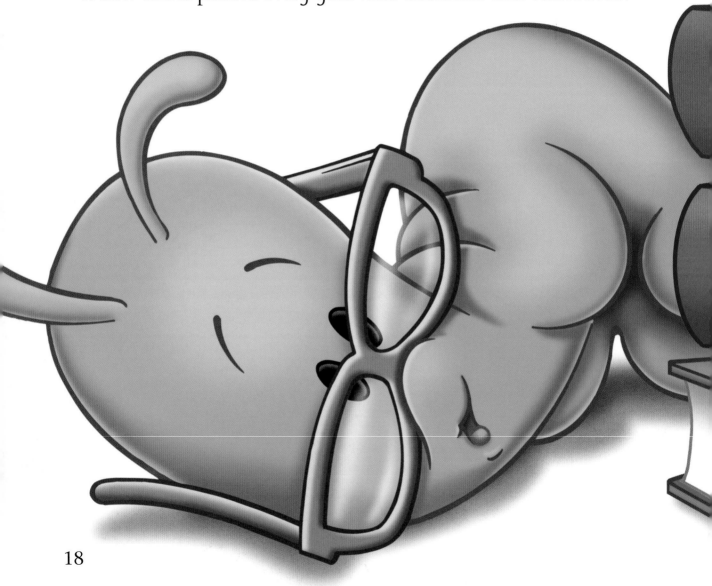

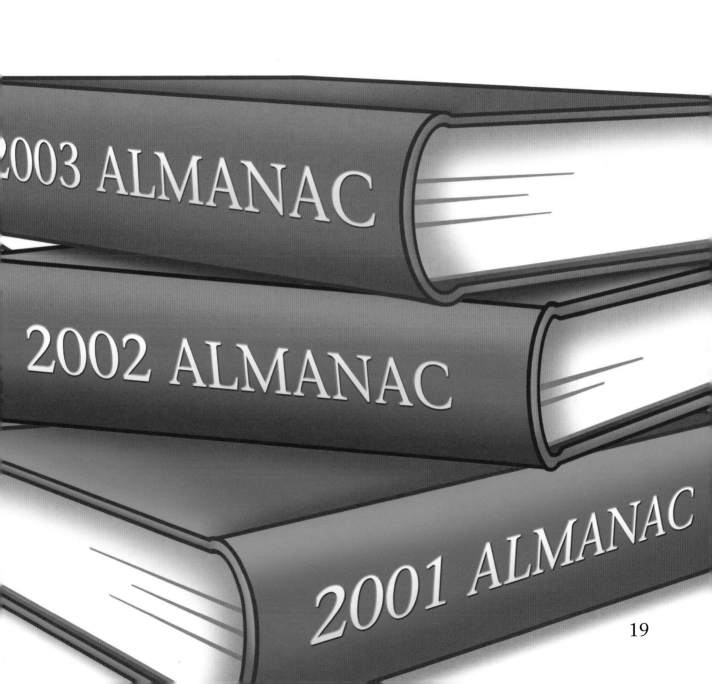

An almanac tells me what I need to know
About populations, disasters, or the most popular TV show.
It's about current events and the world outside.
Pick it up; you'll be surprised at what you'll find inside.

A thesaurus gives suggestions for words that mean the same,
Like *big* and *huge*, *fast* and *quick*, and the nouns *girl* and *dame*.
Opposites are also listed to help define each word.
The thesaurus says that *focused* is an antonym of *blurred*.

Now here are some questions just to see how you do.
To see if you've been listening, let's test your reference I.Q.
Let's see how many reference books you can identify.
Are you ready to think and give it a try?

25

Which book would you use to find the meaning of *knight*?
If you chose the DICTIONARY, you are absolutely right!
Which book would you choose to find a map of the Titanic shipwreck?
If you chose an ATLAS, you're absolutely correct!

Which book would you choose to find a word that is similar to *sweet*?
You got it! A THESAURUS; you can't be beat!
Which book would tell you the population of each state?
Sure, you're right! An ALMANAC; that's positively great!

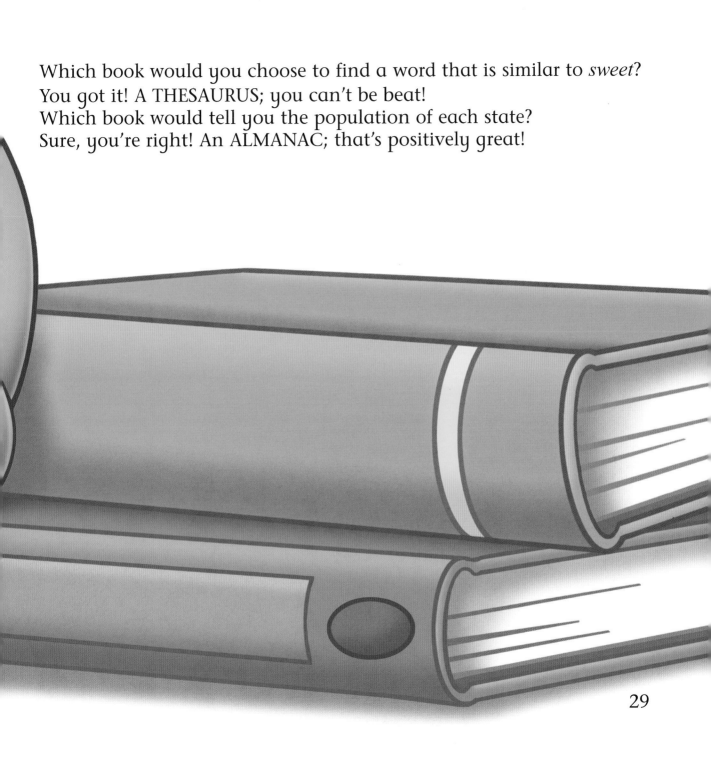

I need to learn about eagles. Now where should I look?
If you said ENCYCLOPEDIA, you chose the right book.
Where should I look for driving directions?
If you said an ATLAS, you need no correction!

In what book might I find information about worms like me?
If you yelled out ENCYCLOPEDIA, I'll give a shout of glee.
You did a great job; now let out a giggle.
You're a reference bookworm, just like Mr. Wiggle!